Thank You,
CROW

by Michael Minkovitz   illustrated by Jose D. Medina

penny
candy
BOOKS

Penny Candy Books
Oklahoma City & Savannah
Text © 2018 Michael Minkovitz
Illustrations © 2018 Jose D. Medina

FSC
MIX
Paper from responsible sources
FSC® C016245
www.fsc.org

This book is printed on paper certified to the environmental and social standards of the Forest Stewardship Council™ (FSC®).

Author & illustrator photo: Autumn Foutz Photography
Design: Shanna Compton

22 21 20 19 18   1 2 3 4 5
ISBN-13: 978-0-9987999-8-8 (hardcover)

Books for the kid in *all* of us
www.pennycandybooks.com

For Carol & Santiago

SEBASTIAN liked to go to his spot in the woods for imaginary adventures and playing pretend.

One day, Sebastian heard
a squawk and a rustle
in a nearby bush.

So he poked it
with a stick,

and out popped

a **crow**!

The crow looked scary,
    but her wing was hurt badly,
        so Sebastian helped.

Crow said,
"SQUAAAAWK!"

and
hopped away.

Across town, a cat grew tired
of his ball of yarn.

He seemed more
interested in other things.

Crow asked politely if she
could have the ball of yarn.

The cat said,
   "Sure, be my guest."

Crow said,
   "SQUAAAAAWK!"
and took to the air.

"You're welcome!"
   meowed the cat.

To Sebastian's surprise,

Crow came back . . .

bearing a gift,

which made Sebastian smile.

Sebastian had no use for a ball of yarn,
but he said thank you anyway.

Crow flew away . . .

and spotted spoons
in the baker's rubbish bin.
She asked politely
if she could have them.

The baker gave a thumbs-up sign.
And Crow said,
"SQUAAAAWK!"

The baker said,
"You're welcome,
Crow!"

Crow clacked away.

To Sebastian's surprise,
Crow came back again

with another gift Sebastian
didn't need, but he said
thank you anyway.

Crow flew to the park and spied a witch with a cone for a hat.

Crow found a hat with a beautiful flower in it, and they made a fair trade.

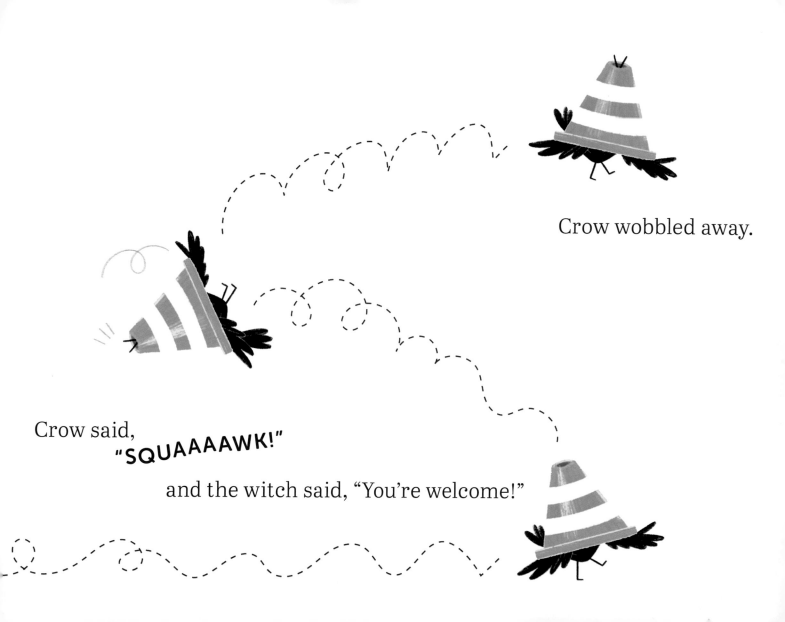

Crow wobbled away.

Crow said,
"SQUAAAAWK!"

and the witch said, "You're welcome!"

To Sebastian's delight,
Crow came back.

Sebastian wasn't sure what he could
do with a traffic cone, but he said
thank you anyway.

Later that day, Crow paid a visit to her old friend the giant who had just finished a giant can of soda.

All giants know that crows like shiny things so he offered the can to Crow.

"SQUAAAAWK!" Crow said.

"You're welcome, Crow!"
said the giant.

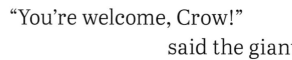

When Crow left again,

Sebastian wondered what weird
thing she would bring back next.

This time, Crow returned with nothing
but a gleam in her eye.

Crow swirled and swooshed in
the trees over the yarn and spoons
and all of the gifts she'd brought.

Turns out,
    her gifts weren't junk at all.

As they blasted off,
Sebastian smiled and yelled,
"Thank you, Crow!"

And Crow said . . .

Jose Medina is an illustrator from Venezuela who now resides in Savannah, Georgia. After beginning his art education in Caracas, he finished his illustration degree at the Savannah College of Art and Design in 2017. His art addresses complex ideas in a way that is simple and engaging, focusing on social and political activism while incorporating humor and lightheartedness. *Thank You, Crow* is Jose's first book, and he was thrilled to work on it with his husband, Michael.

Michael Minkovitz is a Georgia native who gained a unique perspective growing up in the only Jewish family in a tiny, rural community before ending up at New York University's Tisch School, where he graduated with a degree in filmmaking. He later graduated from the Savannah College of Art and Design with a Master's degree in film, but he's also had fun being a news photographer, an SAT tutor, and running his family's business. He is overjoyed to create and publish his first book with his husband, Jose.